cones

ON SITE

By Chris Madeley
Illustrated by Zara Hussain

Fisher King Publishing

Published by
Fisher King Publishing
The Studio
Arthington Lane
Pool-in-Wharfedale
LS21 1JZ
England
www.fisherkingpublishing.co.uk

Conestance, Conerad, and Cone-Vera were dozing in the warm sun. Conen was becoming impatient and woggled off to see what he could find.

Conen returned looking very excited. "Come on sleepy-heads, wake up NOW!" he shouted. "I've found the best place ever to explore! Wait 'til you see it!" They followed Conen and just around the corner was an amazing sight.

There were Cherry Pickers, All Terrain Fork Lifts, Excavators, Dumpers, Diggers, JCBs and Cranes everywhere. "Wow!" Conerad exclaimed, "just look at those – this looks like a really fun place!"

"There are also lots of humans working. We will have to be very careful they don't see us talking together," Cone-Vera warned.

Unfortunately for the four friends, Cone Collector was passing – he was heading for the building site. "What are these four Cones doing here?" he muttered. "On to the truck with you, you can go and work on the building site and be useful." He tossed them up onto the stacks of Cones, got back in his cab and drove into the building site.

Once the truck was inside the perimeter fence, the Cones were thrown off the back of Cone Collector. They stood shivering in the mud.

"Hello and welcome to my building site!" a big voice said.

Cone-Vera turned around. A big Cone wearing a hard hat was standing behind her. "Where are we? What do we have to do?" she said.

"This is a Building Site. It is very dangerous, but very interesting. All of you, follow me. I want to show you something."

NO UNAUTHORISED ACESS
ANYONE WORKING ON OR VISITING THIS SITE

1	MUST	Sign in and out daily at the office/gatehouse.
2	MUST	Recieve a site induction.
3	MUST	Wear a safety helmet, safety footwear and a high visibility vest at all times.
4	MUST	Keep to the defined access routes & comply with the vehicle speed limits.
5	MUST	Know what the risks are from: Their Work Their Materials Their Environment.
6	MUST	Use mechanical means for lifting wherever possible.
7	MUST	Ensure that all edges or openings are fully protected at all times.
8	MUST	Be suitably trained & competent. (CSCS, CPCS etc)
9	MUST	Know the site specific emergency procedures.
10	MUST	Report all accidents and incidents within 20 minutes to the Site Manager.
11	MUST	Not modify Scaffold unless authorised to do so.
12	MUST	Park in the designated parking areas.

IF IN DOUBT - STOP - ASK!

CAUTION
Site
Entrance

The new Cone stopped by a big board. "My name is Conestructor and I make sure this site is safe. Look at this. These are important instructions and information for keeping safe on a building site. It may look fun, but it really is very dangerous and you should **never, ever** even think about playing here."

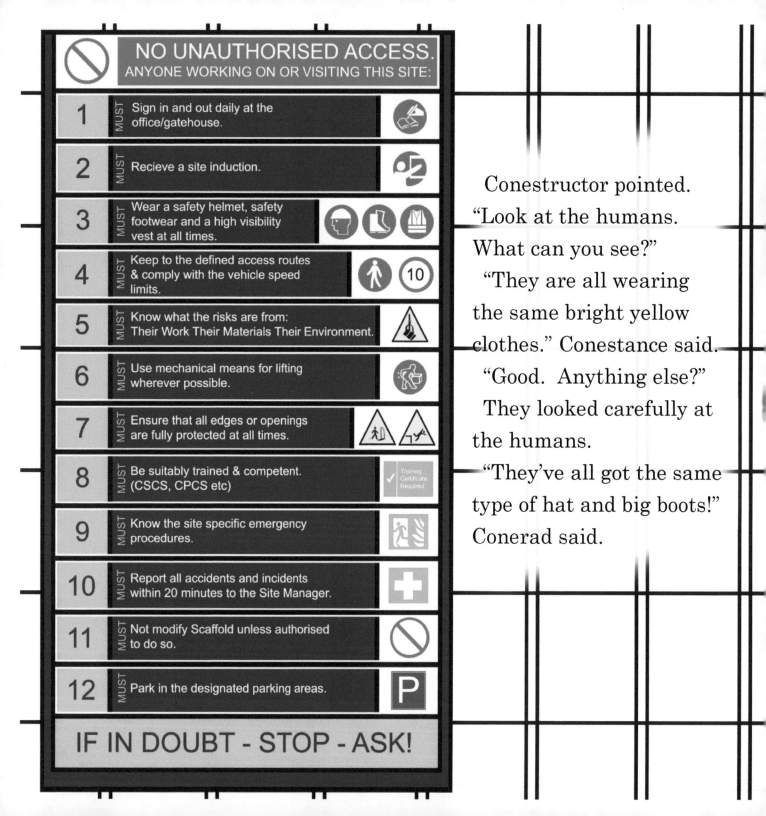

NO UNAUTHORISED ACCESS.
ANYONE WORKING ON OR VISITING THIS SITE:

1. MUST Sign in and out daily at the office/gatehouse.

2. MUST Recieve a site induction.

3. MUST Wear a safety helmet, safety footwear and a high visibility vest at all times.

4. MUST Keep to the defined access routes & comply with the vehicle speed limits.

5. MUST Know what the risks are from: Their Work Their Materials Their Environment.

6. MUST Use mechanical means for lifting wherever possible.

7. MUST Ensure that all edges or openings are fully protected at all times.

8. MUST Be suitably trained & competent. (CSCS, CPCS etc)

9. MUST Know the site specific emergency procedures.

10. MUST Report all accidents and incidents within 20 minutes to the Site Manager.

11. MUST Not modify Scaffold unless authorised to do so.

12. MUST Park in the designated parking areas.

IF IN DOUBT - STOP - ASK!

Conestructor pointed. "Look at the humans. What can you see?"

"They are all wearing the same bright yellow clothes." Conestance said.

"Good. Anything else?"

They looked carefully at the humans.

"They've all got the same type of hat and big boots!" Conerad said.

"Well done." Conestructor said. "This clothing is called PPE, Personal Protective Equipment. They are high visibility so that workers can be seen by anyone driving a big vehicle. The hats are really hard to protect their heads and the boots have hard toe protectors in case things drop on their feet."

"Please, can we go on site if we wear hard hats and high viz jackets?" Conerad asked.

Conestructor nodded. The four friends couldn't fit into protective boots but they put on hard hats and high visibility jackets and followed Conestructor through a gate onto the site.

"What are they building?" Cone-Vera asked.

"This will be a big new shopping centre."

"I love shops!" Conestance said, woggling off. "Wait!" Conestructor said, "you can't just walk across a building site. Look, there's a Cherry Picker coming."

"But, I've got my jacket on, he can see me." Conestance said.

"He can see you but he can't stop a big vehicle quickly. Please stay on the walkway where there is a fence to keep you safe."

"Excuse me," Conestructor said, "I must listen to what Peter the Site Manager is saying to that driver."

As he turned away, Conen said, "let's go and see what we can find." The Cones woggled away.

"No humans! Look, a pile of pallets. We could jump off them," Conen giggled.

"I don't think you should," Cone-Vera said. Too late! Conerad had climbed up the stack and with a wave of his arms, jumped off.

Conerad yelped in pain as he landed.

"What's the matter?" Conestance said, rushing over to him.

"Base... hurts... nail... stuck!" Conerad gasped.

They looked at his base and saw a long, sharp nail sticking out. With a lot of huffing and puffing they pulled it out, but it really hurt poor Conerad.

Conestructor came up to them. "What have you done?" he said. "I told you. Building sites are dangerous. No playing!"

He took the friends towards a building.

"Wow!" Conen said, pointing.

"Stand back!" Conestructor said. "They are moving supports for window frames on the All Terrain Fork Lift."

As Conestance, Cone-Vera, Conen and Conerad watched, they realised just how big the supports were and how easy it would be to get in the way. The four friends moved quickly to one side to keep safe.

The Cones went into the shell of a building. "There are workmen at the other end but they won't see us. They are taking down and moving a roof support," Conestructor explained.

"That looks dangerous," Cone-Vera said. "Look at the sparks!"

"They wear special glasses to protect their eyes from dust and sparks from the metal," Conestructor explained.

They all went outside again.

"Hey, they look fun!" Conen said, pointing to a pile of huge concrete tubes.

"These tubes are drains and are buried deep in the earth. Be careful, Excavator is working here and he digs enormous, deep, long trenches and piles up the earth at the side to put back when the work is done."

The Cones woggled towards the drains. "Whoohoo! A muddy puddle!" Conen yelled. He did a big jump... only it wasn't a puddle. Excavator had been digging a trench for drains and it was full of muddy water. Conen disappeared from sight with a splash.

Conestance, Cone-Vera and Conerad were shocked into silence. After a few seconds, Conen's dirty face reappeared.

"Help! I can't get out! It's sticky and dirty! HELP!"

Conestructor looked horrified. "We must get him out quickly. The water is very dirty – it could make him really ill."

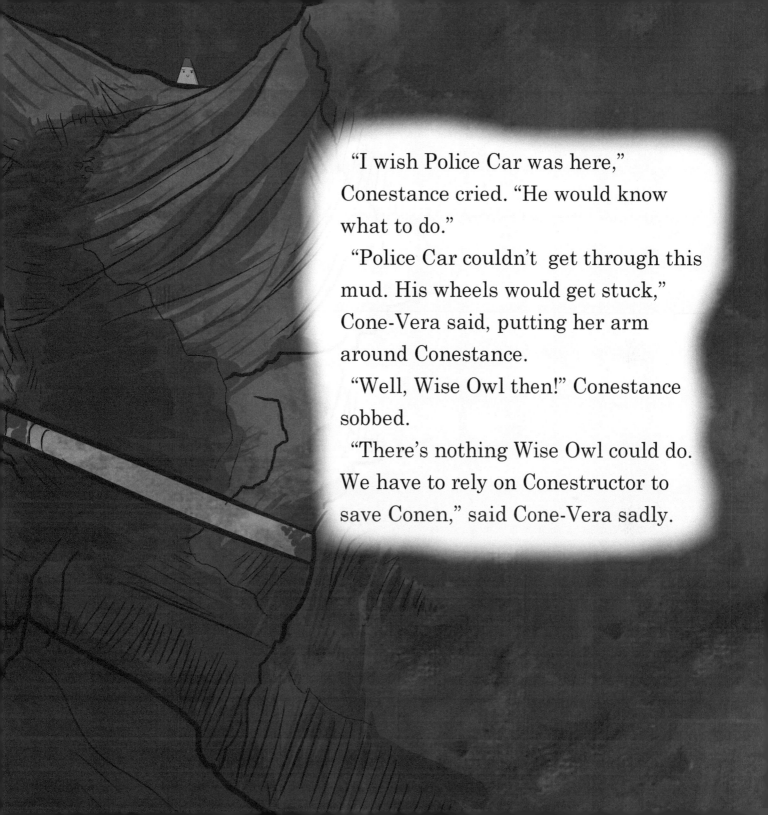

"I wish Police Car was here," Conestance cried. "He would know what to do."

"Police Car couldn't get through this mud. His wheels would get stuck," Cone-Vera said, putting her arm around Conestance.

"Well, Wise Owl then!" Conestance sobbed.

"There's nothing Wise Owl could do. We have to rely on Conestructor to save Conen," said Cone-Vera sadly.

"Hurry up, please!" Conen said. "I'm tired, I might sink."

"Be brave, Conen," Conerad said. "Here comes Conestructor."

Constructor came puffing towards them carrying a thick rope. "Tie this around your middle and hold on tightly. Everyone, when I count to three, pull. One... two... three... PULL."

Conestructor, Conerad, Conestance and Cone-Vera pulled hard. Very slowly, with a nasty, muddy, slurping sound, Conen was pulled to safety.

Cone-Vera was furious with Conen. "You naughty Cone! Don't you ever listen? Conestructor warned us to be careful. Construction sites are DANGEROUS! You could have been killed! Now you're filthy and smell horrible."

Conen hung his head in shame. "I am so very, very sorry, Conestructor. Is there anything else we can see, please? Can we go to see the Cherry Pickers and the big Crane?" Conen looked hopefully at Conestructor.

"All right," he laughed. "I expect you've learned your lesson now. Follow me and **be careful**."

A digger was parked ready to work at a deep excavation. Peter, the Site Manager was instructing the workmen to erect a big fence around the excavation and the digger to keep everyone safe.

"I d..d..don't like it," Conestance said, "it makes my tummy go fluttery and I feel wobbly."

"Come away," Cone-Vera said. A large truck piled high with rubble thundered past and everyone jumped. Conestance screamed and Conerad, Conen and Cone-Vera looked on in horror as she tumbled down to the bottom of a very large hole.

Poor Conestance! Her handbag was wet through, she was dirty and there was mud in her hair.

"Have you got your rope, Conestructor?" Conerad asked.

"No, I left it behind. We must think of another way to rescue her." He scratched his head. "We can't get down there; the sides are too steep. When the humans go for lunch I'll speak to some of the machinery to see if they can help."

Lunchtime came and the workers left the site. Conestructor did as he promised. "Excavator has offered to help with his digger, but that wouldn't be safe. Crane is our best hope as he can move really slowly and gently. He has a chain which he uses to carry heavy loads. Conestance will have to hold on tightly while he carefully lifts her out."

Crane came slowly across the mud from where he had been working. He very carefully extended his arm over the hole. The heavy hook was swinging gently but he was careful not to let it bump into Conestance.

"Hold onto the hook, Conestance, and you will be out in no time," Conestructor said as the hook came within Conestance's reach.

Crane gently set Conestance back down away from the rim of the hole.

"Thank you so much," everyone said.

Conestance was very upset after her fall.

"Look at my handbag! My base and front are all dirty and look at my face."

"We will soon have you clean again," Cone-Vera said and rubbed her face with a tissue.

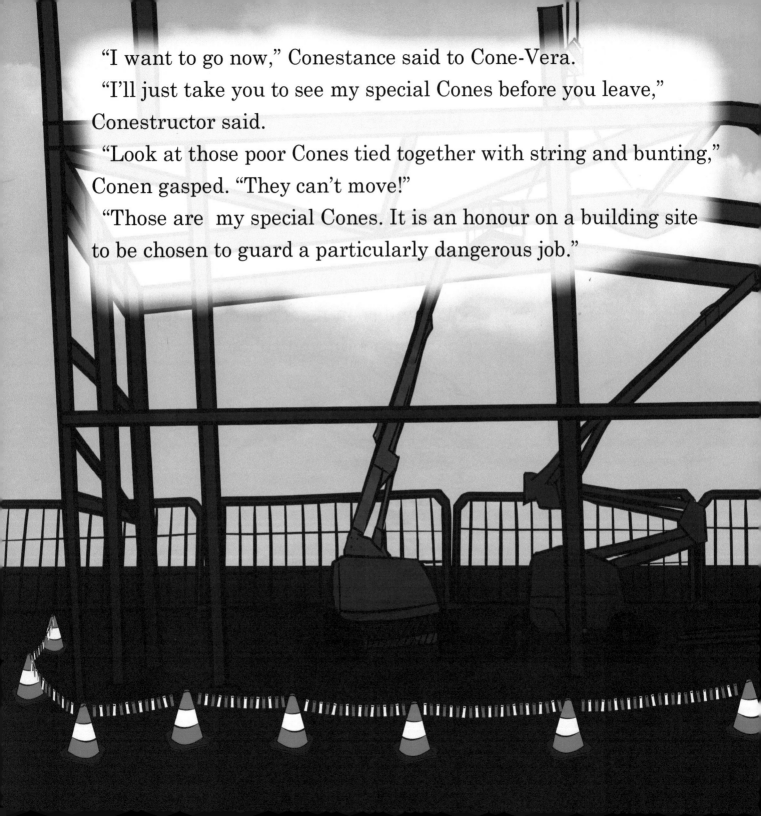

"I want to go now," Conestance said to Cone-Vera.

"I'll just take you to see my special Cones before you leave," Conestructor said.

"Look at those poor Cones tied together with string and bunting," Conen gasped. "They can't move!"

"Those are my special Cones. It is an honour on a building site to be chosen to guard a particularly dangerous job."

"The humans in the Cherry Pickers and Crane are working together to move a roof support into place. It is very dangerous and has to be done slowly to keep the workers safe and to make sure it fits. My special Cones warn all the other site workers that there is a really dangerous job being done so they know to keep away."

When the roof support was safely in place, the Cones decided it was time to go.

"Thank you Conestructor. We have learned so much about keeping safe. We will NEVER, EVER play on a construction site; it's much too dangerous," Cone-Vera said. They woggled away and found some roadworks where they could rest. Police Car, with Wise Owl on the blue lights, came to make sure they were ok.

"Looks like they've had a busy day!" Police Car purred.

"Toohoo Troohooo," Wise Owl replied. "They're a bit muddy, but if they've been with Conestructor for the day they will have learnt some really good lessons about being safe." Wise Owl spread his beautiful wings and flew silently away.

Goodnight Cones, we'll see you again soon for another adventure.

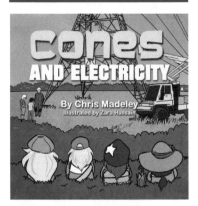

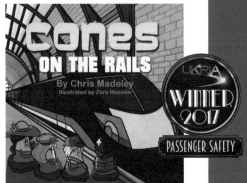

Helping children learn to live and play within parameters based on moral and ethical values.

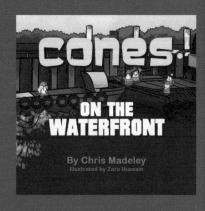

Fun characters having great adventures written to promote:
Being good friends
Embracing differences
Keeping safe
Having lovely manners
Learning who may keep them safe

Join the Cones and enjoy the fun!

Available from all good bookshops and on line, "Meet the Cones" and "Cones Make New Friends" introduces the Cones, how they come alive and how they become friends.

The Cones series of books is written to be fun to read while helping children learn to live with each other in the best possible way but always with safety as their first priority.

CPSIA information can be obtained
at www.ICGtesting.com
Printed in the USA
BVHW022344161121
621634BV00010B/70